SHADOW
PEOPLE

This print edition published in cooperation with Fiction Express, who first published this title in weekly instalments as an interactive e-book.

**FICTI⬤N
EXPRESS**

Fiction Express
First Floor Office, 2 College Street,
Ludlow, Shropshire SY8 1AN
www.fictionexpress.co.uk

Find out more about Fiction Express on pages 129–130.

Design: Laura Durman & Keith Williams
Cover Image: Shutterstock Images

ISBN 978-1-78322-546-0

Printed in Malta by Melita Press.

SHADOW PEOPLE

SHARON GOSLING

What do other readers think?

Here are some comments left on the Fiction Express blog about this book:

"I think Shadow People *is awesome."*
T.Q., Bristol

"I think that the book Shadow People *will have a massive hit when it is published. It has inspired me to read more in an enjoyable way."*
Sebastien, Rochdale

"This book just gets better and better!"
Madamglitter, Redditch

"I really love the [story]. The chapters… really [keep me] on edge and I can't wait for the next chapter."
Neil, London

"OMG! Shadow People *is amazing!"*
Isra, Walsall

Contents

Chapter 1

Shadows in the Air

Alex held his phone as steady as he could and pressed the camera button. There was a tiny clicking sound. One of them stopped and turned around, looking right at him. He froze for a second. Then, breathing hard, Alex fled down the alleyway and skidded into a grimy, narrow street that ran behind the high street shops. It was hardly ever used, except for occasional deliveries. He zigzagged through the messy shadows, heart banging so hard against his ribcage it felt as if it might burst. He dodged an abandoned trolley, his school bag hitting it with a clang that echoed like tinny thunder around the high walls.

Alex risked a glance behind him. There was nothing there. They hadn't followed him. Maybe they hadn't seen him after all.

After stopping to catch his breath, he headed back to the high street. It had begun to rain – cold, fat drops soaking his thin jacket as he crept to the corner and peered around it. There was no sign of them. The shadow people had vanished, like they always did… as if they'd never even been there.

With one last deep breath, Alex headed for the bus stop. He sat down on the narrow bench under the shelter, pulled his mobile phone from his pocket and opened the photograph he'd just taken. Attaching the image, he wrote a text message to his best mate, Jason:

Look! Proof I'm not crazy! This is one of those shadow people I've been telling you about. Now you have to believe me!!

He pressed send, then opened up the notepad app on his phone, starting a new page.

Friday, 9 November, 6:26 pm
Just saw some more shadow people in the high street. Still fuzzy but thought they looked sort of brighter, stronger somehow. I managed to get a pic of one on my phone this time. As soon as I did, the nearest one turned and looked right at me. I really thought he'd seen me. Ran down the alley, but he didn't follow, so maybe he hadn't after all.

Alex saved the note and flicked back through some of the previous ones.

He'd been keeping this diary for the last couple of weeks, recording every sighting of the shadow people. At first they were really faint, like wraiths of fog that often hung around the town. But when he'd commented on them to other people, no one else could see what he was pointing at. That's when he knew something weird was going on. Then they'd started getting clearer…and bigger.

After a while, Alex had realized they were people-shaped – they had heads and arms and legs, although he could never see the details clearly. It was as if they were standing behind marbled glass, or something. For a while Alex had wondered if they were ghosts, but somehow he knew they weren't. They moved too deliberately, as if everything they did had a reason behind it. He'd tried telling Jason about them, once, but his friend had just looked at him as if he was crazy, so he started keeping the diary instead.

A loud 'Beep! Bee-eep!' made him jump, and he looked up to see that the bus had stopped and was waiting for him. He ran to get on it before the driver gave up and drove off. But, as he settled into the back seat and reached for his phone, he realized it wasn't in his bag. He must have dropped it as he ran for the bus.

He turned and looked back along the road, out of the rain-spattered window. The bus shelter was disappearing into the gloom of evening, but he could see his phone, lying abandoned on the ground. Then, as he watched, a girl appeared. She had tight dark curls that fell to her shoulders and wore a plain grey tracksuit.

She was carrying a large black backpack. She looked about Alex's age, but he didn't recognize her from school. She walked towards the bus shelter and picked up Alex's phone, checking it out.

"Hey!" Alex shouted, "Hey – that's mine!"

She didn't hear him, of course. The girl looked around for a moment and then slipped the phone into her pocket before sauntering off.

"Hey!" Alex yelled again, banging hard on the glass. The bus screeched to a halt as the driver pulled over. He opened the door to the bus and climbed out of his cabin.

"What's going on back there?" he shouted at Alex.

"No time to explain… but thanks for stopping!" Alex cried, dashing past him and jumping onto the wet pavement outside. He ran back towards the bus stop, his feet sloshing in the puddles as he went.

But when he got there, the girl – and his phone – were nowhere to be seen.

* * *

"What's up with you then?" Jason asked, as they walked home from school the next day.

"Nothing," muttered Alex.

"Yeah, right," said Jason. "You've been in a right mood all day. It wasn't my text last night, was it?"

Alex looked up. "What text?"

"You know, after you sent me that rubbish photo of the high street."

"I didn't get it," Alex said, gloomily. "I lost my phone last night." Then he realized what Jason had just said. "Wait – what do you mean, rubbish photo?"

Jason shrugged. "You sent me a picture of the high street, going on about these shadow people of yours again."

"But – that was the whole point," Alex said, a strange feeling creeping over him. "That's why I sent you the photo – it was a picture of one of them!"

His friend stopped and pulled his phone out of his pocket. He opened Alex's text and held it out. "See? Nothing there but the rain."

Alex stared at the photo he'd taken. He could see the shadow person. It was right there, a weird bright blur in the middle of the screen. "You can't see that?"

Jason rolled his eyes, "Argh, don't start that again, mate. Joke's over – it didn't work. Leave it at that."

Alex knew when his friend was

pretending, and this wasn't one of those times. Jason really couldn't see it. What did that mean? Was it only Alex? Was he the only person in the world who knew the shadow people were there? Or was he going mad?

"Come on mate, snap out of it!" said Jason, waving a hand in front of his face.

"Sorry," was all Alex could say.

"It's all right," said Jason, cheerily. "You coming for a game of football?"

"Um, nah, I've got stuff to do at home," Alex replied miserably.

"Ok, well I'll see you tomorrow then," Jason called as he headed off towards the playing fields.

"Yeah, see you," Alex replied. He wandered along the path that ran beside the old abandoned industrial estate. Warning signs hung from the bordering fences, saying things like, "Danger! Do Not Enter," but Alex had seen them too many time to take any notice of them and besides, he was too busy thinking about other, more important, things. Such as, for example, why on earth he was seeing things that other people couldn't.

Chapter 2

Finders Keepers

As he carried on walking, thinking about
the shadows, Alex slowly became aware
of a sound growing around him. It started
like a distant *tik-tik-tik* surrounded by
a rush of air. It quickly grew louder and
nearer, a dull growl that seemed to be
swelling to fill the entire sky. Soon the
tik-tik-tik became a deep *WHUMP-
WHUMP-WHUMP* that pounded
through Alex's chest.

A helicopter, thought Alex excitedly as the
aircraft came into view over some trees.

The helicopter was huge, a mottled grey-green bulk with rotors at both ends. It was one of the Chinooks Alex had seen on the news. He always watched those reports, just in case he saw his dad in the background. Alex's dad was a soldier and he hadn't been home for a long time.

As Alex looked on, the helicopter began to lose altitude, skimming the tops of the tall red brick factory towers inside the fence. He realized it was going to land.

Keen to take a closer look, Alex ducked through a section of broken fence, ignoring yet another warning sign, and scrambled down a short bank onto the patchy grass below. He ran around the main factory building, stumbling along the remains of an overgrown concrete path.

As he rounded the corner, he saw the Chinook dropping lower and lower as the pilot guided it in to land. The wind from the blades was so strong it sent dust rising in waves that crashed against the empty buildings.

Alex had to hold his arm up over his eyes to stop them filling with grit. He crouched behind a pile of junk and peered out as the helicopter finally came to a stop, its rotors still turning.

Almost immediately, the door in the side of the helicopter opened. Alex expected a stream of soldiers to appear, but instead, only one figure jumped out. One small, lone figure, dressed in a grey tracksuit with a black pack on its back...

The girl from the bus shelter! Alex realized with a jolt, as another movement caught his eye. It was pretty far away, but he saw a telltale faint white glow moving slowly along the wall – a shadow person!

Alex was distracted as the helicopter began to rise, the spinning blades heaving it into the sky like some huge airborne whale. The girl didn't seem at all bothered about being left behind – she was tapping away at something in her hand. It looked like some sort of tablet.

A moment later, she glanced up, shoved the gadget into her bag and then headed off in the direction of the shadow. Alex searched for the glow, but couldn't see it. It seemed to have vanished completely.

This can't be a coincidence, can it? Alex thought. *The helicopter – and that weird girl – showing up in the same place and the same time as one of those things? They must be connected, surely.*

He watched as the girl ran towards one of the factory buildings. When she reached the door, she held out her arm, waving it over the rusting metal, all the while staring at something on her wrist. From this distance, Alex couldn't make out what it was. Then she opened the door and disappeared inside.

Alex dodged around the pile of junk that had been his hiding place and ran out across the car park towards the building, creeping quietly inside.

A concrete staircase zigzagged above his head. He could see her dusty footprints on the steps and started up after them. As he reached the top, he could hear the girl shouting, her voice faint through a closed wooden door. He pushed against it and the old blue paint flaked off under his hands. But it opened, swinging back to reveal a large office, long ago abandoned.

The door clanged shut again as he slipped through it.

Alex could see the girl on the far side of the room. She had her back to him, one arm raised to her mouth, and she seemed to be talking to herself.

"Oi!" Alex shouted, his voice echoing against the bare walls.

The girl stopped and quickly turned to look straight at him, her face lit by a faint glow that blinked out as she made a swift gesture with her hand.

"You," Alex said, walking nearer. "I saw you last night, at the bus stop. You stole my phone."

The girl tilted her head to one side and crossed her arms. "I didn't steal it," she said, and he was surprised by her American accent. "You lost it. Finders keepers, losers weepers, right, Alex?"

He stopped, astonished.

The girl sighed. "You're not seriously surprised I know your name? I've got your phone, remember?"

"Who are you?" asked Alex. "I saw you get out of that helicopter."

"Yeah, we tracked an incursion to this spot."

Something cold slid down Alex's spine. "A what?"

The girl looked him up and down. "The shadow people you were keeping notes about on your phone. You don't know what they are, do you?"

"Can you see them?" Alex asked. "I thought maybe it was just me."

The girl laughed, but it wasn't a happy sound. "Yeah, I can see them. You, me and four others can – that's all, in the whole world. Well, so far as we know, anyway."

"What are they?" Alex asked.

She clenched her fist, and he noticed the device strapped to her wrist. It was like a smart watch, only chunkier and hexagonal in shape. Suddenly, it began to beep. The girl held up her arm and pressed a button. Something shimmered on the black surface. Alex realized it was a projection – a tiny hologram in the shape of a boy with brown hair and an anxious face. He gave the girl a sharp salute.

"Ellison, report," barked the girl.

"You'd better get him out of there. We've just picked up five more incursions in your vicinity. They're closing in. The extraction team's on its way."

"Where?"

"Ground level is compromised. It'll have to be the roof."

"Got it. Asimov out." The girl pressed another button and the hologram disappeared. "We have to go – now!"

"Wait," Alex said, "You still haven't told me what's going on!"

She turned to him impatiently. "Those things. They're not shadows. They're aliens. They're trying to invade our planet, and there are only six people in the world – including you – who can see them. And thanks to that picture you sent of them last night, they've noticed you. So if I were you, I would trust me and just *RUN*!"

The girl grabbed his arm and dragged him towards the exit, but as they got there a shadow person appeared through the closed door. They slid to a halt, just inches away, and turned to run back the way they had come.

"There's got to be another way out," the girl yelled.

Alex spotted another door in the opposite corner. "There!" he shouted, glancing over his shoulder to see that there were now two shadows in the room. They seemed more solid than ever before. For the first time, Alex could almost make out their faces. They were long and stretched, their empty eyes too big for the rest of their heads, their noses one big vacant hole. They were horrible, and they were getting closer!

The girl got to the door first. It was a fire exit with a safety handle. She rammed it down and it burst open, straight out onto a fire escape. They crashed up the steps towards the roof, feet ringing on the slippery metal. Alex looked down to see another shadow coming up the staircase to join the two behind them. They were moving fast. They were catching up!

"I've got a bead on three," the girl yelled into her wrist device. "Where are the other two? And where's the damn extraction team?"

Alex heard the helicopter and whipped his head around, looking for it, but that made him trip. His feet slid off the metal grille, plunging him over the side. He crashed into the handrail and managed to get his elbows over it, hanging on as his legs dangled into nothing.

"Alex!" The girl leapt back down the steps and pulled him up, pushing him in front of her. "Come on! *Come on!*"

He lunged up the stairs, the shadows so close that he was convinced they'd grab them both at any moment. They reached the roof and saw the helicopter hovering at the edge of the building, its hatch hanging open.

"What are they doing?" he yelled over the noise. "Why haven't they landed?"

"The roof's not strong enough!" the girl yelled back. "We'll have to jump!"

Alex shook his head. "I can't!"

The girl shoved him in the back. "You can! *Do it!*"

Two more shadows appeared out of nowhere, advancing from the other end of the roof. They were surrounded – there was no way out except the helicopter.

"Alex," the girl said, "you can do this. If you don't, they'll take you and I don't know if we'll be able to get you back! I don't know what they'll do to you!"

He shook his head. "I don't even know who you are!"

"My name's Sasha," she yelled back. "And right now, I'm the best friend you've ever had! Now JUMP!"

Alex looked at the gap between the roof and the helicopter. The pilot was doing his best to keep the aircraft steady, but it was still moving. The ground below was a long, long way off.

"Don't look down," said the girl. "Just do it!"

"You go first," he said. "I'll follow!"

She didn't hesitate, running straight at the edge of the roof and sailing through the air. She hit the helicopter's floor and rolled to her feet, turning to face him.

"Come on!" She screamed. "Alex! Come on! Jump now!"

Chapter 3

Different Dimensions

Alex stared at the gap between the edge of the building and the hovering helicopter. It looked about as long as the sofa at home – probably a couple of metres. He tried to remember if he'd ever jumped that far before.

"Alex!" Sasha yelled. "Come on – jump! You've got to do it!"

He turned to glance behind him and got the shock of his life. The shadow people were really close. He could see the shape of their weird long heads through the blur of white around them. Fear forced him into movement. Whipping his head back around he looked at the gap again. He could make that! Of course he could, it wasn't that far.

"Alex," Sasha screamed again. "Now!"

He shut his eyes, took two steps back as a run up and–

Something cold snaked around his arm. It felt like a rope, but when he looked down he couldn't see anything. Alex ran towards the roof's edge, but the thing on his wrist pulled tight, jerking him backwards. He tried to pull away from the invisible rope, but found that he couldn't move. He felt an intense cold spreading through him, from his arm all the way up to the top of his head and down to his feet. His body froze. It felt a bit like when he opened the big chest freezer in the garage and the cold air rolled over him.

Except this went deeper, right to his bones, and it didn't pass.

He was frozen solid in his own body, stretched out on tip-toe as if still taking a run-up for the biggest jump of his life. The really weird thing was that the rest of the world was still moving. He could see the helicopter bobbing slightly, its rotors still spinning. There was Sasha, frantically waving her arms and shouting, trying to get him to run.

I can't, Alex wanted to yell, but he couldn't get his mouth to form the words.

Everything around him began to shiver. Blood rushed in his ears and the world just – disappeared. Not quickly, in a blink, but gradually and from the edges of his vision. It began to move like a whirlwind. Alex felt as if he were spinning, faster and faster, until the world around him was nothing but a blur, getting further and further away.

And then it was gone.

* * *

Alex woke up to find himself flat on his back. He blinked, almost blinded by the hard white light overhead. Taking a gasping breath, he coughed as a weird acrid smell caught in the back of his throat. The sound echoed back at him, and with it came another noise he hadn't registered before. A low whispering that moved closer and then faded away again, over and over, like waves rolling over a beach.

As his eyes adjusted to the bright light, Alex began to realize that something was moving around him. Or, more accurately, some *things* were moving around him – shapes at the edges of the room, beyond the light so he couldn't see them properly. He tried to work out where he was. Had he jumped, and made it into the helicopter? Had he knocked himself out and ended up in hospital, or something? Then he remembered the cold thing snaking around his arm.

Was he still frozen? Alex tried lifting his hand. At first it seemed easy enough and relief rushed through him – but then something tugged at his wrist, holding it down. He wriggled his legs, too, but there was something around each ankle. He wasn't paralysed any more but his arms and legs were restrained by something like handcuffs.

Fear gripped Alex as he struggled, realizing that he wasn't on the floor, as he'd first thought, but on a narrow table. He felt it move slightly as he tried to wrench himself free.

"Help!" He yelled. His voice sounded hoarse as the smell nearly choked him again. "Help! Help – anyone? Sasha? Help!"

The shapes at the edge of the room moved forward into the light. He was surrounded by shadow people, only now they weren't just shadows. For the first time, Alex could see them properly.

He screamed and struggled again as they inched closer, but he couldn't break free.

Their skin was pale, not white but a kind of pearl-grey, almost transparent. They were tall, and everything about them seemed to be gangly – their arms and legs were much longer than a human's. Their faces were terrifying – like expressionless masks out of which blinked huge, black, bug-like eyes. Their mouths were creepy – round, beak-like things that opened and shut, as if they were talking all the time but not actually saying anything.

One of them reached a long, bony hand towards him. Alex noticed that it had seven fingers – although they looked more like talons, with sharp, hooked claws at the tip. He tried to turn away, but couldn't. It came closer and closer, until finally it pressed one finger sharply against his forehead…

…and everything went black.

* * *

The next time Alex woke, he really was on the floor. There was a light coming from somewhere, much dimmer than the last one. He was in a different room… and this time, he could move.

Alex hauled himself up into a sitting position and looked around. He was clearly in some sort of cage made of thick hexagonal wire, like a steel honeycomb. Beyond this, he could make out other cages, all connected in a long line as far as he could see.

He stretched out his legs, and clunked his foot against one of two heavy silver-coloured bowls that were on the floor beside him. One was full of clear liquid that looked like water, and the other held something that resembled very milky porridge. Alex realized he was really thirsty. He hesitated – would it be safe to drink something… *alien*?

"It's all right," came a voice, behind his left shoulder. "You can drink it. It's water."

Alex stood up and spun around to see another boy looking at him through the cage wall.

"You can eat the other stuff, too, if you want," the boy added. "It's gross, but it's not poisonous."

"Who are you?" Alex asked as he gulped the water, a million questions bursting into his mind, along with relief at finding himself not alone. "Where – where did you come from? What happened to you? Where are we? What–"

"Whoa!" The boy held up his hands. "Slow down! I'm Zhou. Who are you?"

"Alex," said Alex.

"Ahh, Alex – I've heard of you. Shadow People, and all that," said Zhou, nodding. "Looks like Sasha didn't get to you in time, eh? I'm sorry."

Alex sank down again, his brain throbbing. "Are you part of her team?" Alex asked.

"Yup," said the boy. "Task Force Alpha. The greys got me yesterday."

"Greys?" Alex asked, faintly.

Zhou shrugged. "Greys is just the default name the military gives to any alien species. Although now I'm here, I think you're right. 'Shadows' is a better name!"

"Where *are* we?" Alex asked again.

"Well, that's complicated," said Zhou. "As far as I can tell, we're on a spaceship. A really, *really* big one. Where exactly we are, though… I think we're in another dimension. What do you remember about the moment they grabbed you?"

Alex thought back. "I don't know… it was all a bit blurry. It felt as if I was being sucked into a tornado."

Zhou nodded. "Right. Me too. See, I think that was us being hauled from one dimension to another. Through a wormhole, or something."

"But what – what do you mean, 'another dimension'?"

Zhou shrugged. "We think there are other dimensions that we don't know about – probably more than one universe. They're all lined up next to ours, like separate floors of an infinite tower block. Every one is different, and there aren't supposed to be staircases between the floors. We're all supposed to stay on our own. But these greys – the aliens – they're building a way through, somehow. They're knocking through the ceiling into our floor. They haven't made the hole big enough for them all to get through yet…"

Alex finished the sentence for him. "… But it's getting bigger every day," he said.

"Right," agreed Zhou, "They obviously haven't quite worked out how to get to Earth properly yet. Not their whole army, anyway – and, thankfully, not this ship. But they're getting closer…"

Alex felt a bit sick. "I don't understand any of this. What do they want with you and me?"

"Experimentation, of course. They want to know how we tick, and how we can see them. They thought they were invisible to humans, but you and me – and the rest of Task Force Alpha – we can see them. If it weren't for us, they could have just suddenly invaded Earth at full strength, before any of us had a chance to stop them. But now – now they know that there's a chance we might be ready for them."

Alex peered around. "Is anyone else here?"

"Nope," said Zhou, cheerily. He pulled something out of his pocket. It was a penknife. "And thankfully for both of us, the aliens don't seem to know what pockets are. Which has been very useful – I've found a way out!"

He passed the penknife through the bars, and began fiddling with the door. A second later he was out of his own cage and standing in front of Alex's.

"You have to look really hard, but there are tiny screws here down the side – the same principle as ours on Earth," Zhou explained, pointing. "They're hard to loosen, but you can do it. Quick – we've got to get out of here."

"I'm not sure about this," said Alex, following Zhou's instructions. "Even if we make it out of here, what can we do then? There are only two of us!"

"We can find a way back to Earth with lots of valuable intelligence about this ship," said the other boy. "Come on – *hurry*!"

"But – but we might get caught. And you said this ship was massive," protested

Alex. "It's not like we'll be able to remember all of it."

"Would you rather I left you here for them to experiment on?" Zhou asked.

"No!" Alex gasped.

"Well, what did I say about aliens and pockets? I've got my phone – I can take pictures, and if we can find a map of the ship…."

"This is crazy," said Alex, furiously undoing the screws. "This can't be real. Is this one of those TV programmes? Like – where they make you think the world has ended when really it's just your mum wanting you to get out of bed on time in the mornings? Is this all a trick?"

"You wish," said Zhou. "Come on – *hurry*! Sooner or later they're going to come for us again."

Alex wrenched the last screw around one more time and pulled it out. Zhou pushed against the door and it lifted clean away.

"Follow me," said Zhou, in a low voice.

Chapter 4

Out of the Frying Pan...

Zhou and Alex crept quietly but quickly through the dim light until they reached a door. It was large and metal, with a complicated opening mechanism that Zhou made easy work of. Beyond was another, larger corridor, also empty. Zhou didn't hesitate, turning left and moving quickly along the hallway. He peered through every door they passed as if he were carefully assessing everything inside.

"What are you looking for?" Alex whispered.

"Computer terminal," Zhou whispered back. "So we can hack into their mainframe."

Alex frowned. "How will you know how to use it?"

Zhou glanced at him and grinned. "I've got an app for that."

"But—"

Zhou held up a hand and they both stopped. They'd reached another doorway. Inside this one was a large room with booths built into the walls. In each was a pedestal with something that looked a bit like a keyboard and a thin, flat screen.

They slipped inside, going to one of the booths. Zhou pulled out his phone. "It's something special the military developed for us," he explained quietly, unsnapping a compartment in the back of the phone and pulling out a long, thin cable. "All I need to do is plug it in. Then the app will do three things – broadcast a homing beacon, so Task Force Alpha knows where we are; download schematics... plans of the ship," Zhou explained seeing Alex's frown, "and it'll search for an escape route."

He located the interface under the 'keyboard', a small hexagonal opening with several spikes inside it. Zhou held up the phone's cable so Alex could see. Instead of the standard connector, the cable had a bulbous black end. Zhou pressed it into the alien interface, and Alex watched, amazed, as it moulded itself to the aperture.

"Malleable conductive polymer. It interfaces with anything," Zhou explained, as he tapped an app icon on his phone screen. "Neat, huh?"

The alien computer burst into life as Zhou's programme did its work. They watched as screen after screen flashed up as it sought the information they needed.

"Well, the homing beacon's activated," Zhou said, a moment later. "No idea if it'll reach Earth, but better something than nothing…."

Suddenly, the alien computer froze mid-flash, and then the screen blacked out completely.

"Uh-oh," said Zhou.

A loud, piercing siren started up, followed by a mechanical whine coming from behind them. Alex looked to see the door of the computer room slowly shutting, trapping them in.

"Run," he yelled, leaping out of the booth and heading for the door as Zhou tried to disconnect his phone. Alex made it first, crashing through the narrow gap and out into the corridor. Zhou stumbled as he ran and Alex tried to stop the door closing, pulling on it with all his might, but it was so heavy it was useless. Zhou reached the door and hesitated. The gap was already tight.

"Quickly," Alex hissed, "Zhou–"

Zhou breathed in and slid through the opening. It was now so small that he almost got stuck. Alex grabbed his arm and pulled, dragging Zhou to safety. The door crunched home with just milliseconds to spare.

From somewhere distant came the noise of something hard banging against metal – thump, thump, thump, thump. Alex knew instantly what it was. He'd seen his dad's regiment at parades. It was an army, marching in quick time – and it was advancing on them.

"We've got to hide," he said. "Where can we go?"

"There's no point staying in the corridors," Zhou said, "They'll have us surrounded!"

He pointed at a hatch low in the wall. It was tiny – a vent of some sort – far too small for a grey to get into, but perhaps big enough for them. They had no choice. Together they wrenched off the metal cover. Alex pushed himself inside, head first. The space was so narrow that he had to lie flat on his stomach and crawl, pulling himself forward by his forearms. He heard the faint clang as Zhou replaced the vent cover behind them.

"Keep going," Zhou whispered.

Alex shut his eyes, feeling claustrophobic. What if the tunnel got narrower, instead of wider? He'd get stuck! He took a deep breath and crawled forward some more.

At least the aliens can't follow us in here, he reassured himself. *There's no way they'd fit.*

It seemed like an age later that Alex suddenly felt as if he could breathe more freely. He looked around to see that they'd reached an intersection in the vents – four joining together. It gave them a little more space. He stopped, turning so that he could draw his knees up and lean against the vent wall. Zhou was right behind him.

"Right," said the other boy, pulling his phone out again. "Let's see what we managed to get."

Alex leaned over to watch as Zhou swiped through page after page of downloaded information and maps of the ship. Then he stopped, went back one screen, and zoomed in. The image seemed to show a series of little circles grouped around a central double line that looked a bit like a corridor.

"Well, hello," he said.

"What?" Alex asked. "What is that?"

"Our escape route. I think they're space pods. If we can get to one of those babies, we can get off this ship."

Alex stared.

"And go where? You said we were in a different dimension!"

Zhou nodded. "Yeah. But they've got a wormhole, remember? I told you – a hole they're knocking through to our universe. There's no reason why we can't find it."

Alex shook his head. "That's insane. Do you even know how to fly a 'space pod'? And don't," he said, holding up a hand as Zhou opened his mouth to speak, "tell me 'you've got an app for that'."

Chapter 5

Close Call

"Well?" said Alex.

Zhou looked at him seriously. "We've got to get off this ship. I say our best chance is to head for the space pods. I'm sure I can work out how to fly one."

Alex stared at him. He thought it was crazy, but he could also remember the feeling of being clamped down on that metal bed with a horrible-looking grey coming towards him. He shivered. He didn't want to go through that again. What other choice did they have?

"Okay," Alex said. "Let's do it."

Zhou grinned. "Right answer," he said.

They took a left fork at the next air vent junction and carried on crawling. Alex hated being inside the narrow metal tube.

Every time they passed a vent, Zhou insisted on stopping to assess whatever lay on the other side. "We need intelligence," he whispered, when Alex complained that they were wasting time. "Task Force Alpha has never had this kind of opportunity before."

"It won't do much good if we get caught before we can give it to them, will it?" Alex grumbled.

"We're almost there," Zhou said, after they'd been crawling for what felt like hours. "There are just two more forks, and–" he stopped.

"And what?" Alex asked, trying to look back over his shoulder. Zhou had stopped at yet another grille and was staring through it.

"Look," Zhou whispered, pointing.

Alex managed to shuffle around enough to stick his head next to Zhou's. Through the vent opening he could see a narrow corridor. Beyond that was an open door into another room crammed full of complicated computer equipment. Two greys were standing there, discussing something. Every now and then one of them would press a button and point. The other would nod, as if in agreement.

"Let's get out of here," said Alex. "Just looking at them gives me the creeps."

"Wait," whispered Zhou. He took out his phone and positioned it against the grille so that the camera was between the gaps. Alex saw him shift from camera to video and start recording.

As they watched, one of the greys moved to stand a little way from the other, in the middle of the room. The one still at the console looked up, as if waiting for confirmation that the other was ready for something. When that grey nodded, it pressed a series of buttons. Alex saw Zhou zoom in to catch his actions.

Both boys jumped as a blue light filled the room. It came from a pinprick whirlpool-like blur that appeared in mid-air. It spun, white energy flickering around its edge, growing larger, until it was the size of a grey itself. The alien standing in the middle of the room stepped forward – right into the blue light – and vanished completely. The grey controlling the console looked at something on a screen, nodded once, and pressed another button. The light disappeared as if it had never been there. The remaining grey left the room and walked away down the corridor, leaving the two boys in silence.

"That's it," said Zhou, turning off the video. "That's them, breaking through into our dimension. We just watched one of them crossing over."

Alex looked at Zhou's phone. "And you videoed it."

Zhou nodded, seeming a little dazed. He clenched his jaw. "I need to get closer. Take more photographs."

"You're not thinking of going out there?" Alex asked, aghast. "You're insane! What if you get caught?"

"This is too important an opportunity to miss," said Zhou. "This could be the answer to saving Earth."

"But–" Alex protested, but it was too late. Zhou was already undoing the screws that held the vent in place. He crawled out and stopped for a second, looking both ways down the corridor and listening.

Zhou dashed quickly and quietly into the room, phone at the ready. Alex held his breath as he snapped a few pictures. Two minutes later he was back, his face still serious. "Let's go," he said, quickly replacing the vent grille. "It's vital we get this back to base."

Zhou crawled away in front of him. Alex followed on his heels – he didn't want to get lost in here on his own.

"This is it," Zhou whispered, a short time later. "We're here."

He was sitting beside another vent grille. This one had a much wider space around it and Zhou beckoned for Alex to look. Outside, they could see a sort of hangar deck or docking station. It was huge –

four storeys of open space with balconies running around each level and metal steps leading up from the floor.

"Those are the pods," Zhou said, pointing to a series of round metal plates set in the wall of each level. Each had a circular handle in the centre, a little like a steering wheel. "Or the airlocks that lead to the pods, anyway. We have to turn one of those handles and step through it. The pod itself is set right in the side of the ship, so that part of it is out in space. Like… like a pea sticking out of a pile of mash. When we detach, it'll drop out into zero gravity and then we can fly away."

"How do you know all that?" Alex asked.

Zhou held up his phone. On the screen was a schematic showing the hangar they were looking at now, but in cross-section, so they could also see the outer hull of the spaceship. Sure enough, there were little circles half in and half out of the ship.

"Okay," he said. "So what do we do?"

Zhou peered around. "I can't see any greys, can you?"

Alex shook his head. "No. They must be there somewhere, though."

Zhou shrugged. "At least we've got the element of surprise. Come on – we just have to be quick. We'll head for the nearest pod – on the first level, closest to us. Ready?"

Alex took a deep breath. "You really think you can fly one of these things?"

Zhou nodded, but didn't grin, which somehow made Alex even more nervous. "We have to do this, Alex. It's the only way out. If Task Force Alpha were going to send a rescue, they'd be here by now."

Alex knew he was right. "Let's do it," he said.

They undid the vent and slipped out into the empty, still-humming corridor. It was cold in the hangar, far colder than anywhere else they'd been on the ship. They ran across the deck, and Alex saw Zhou glancing this way and that for any sign of aliens, but there was none. They got to the stairs and raced up them, making for the closest pod. It seemed much larger close up than it had from a distance.

"Help me turn this," Zhou whispered, grasping one side of the circular handle. "After three, ready? One, two, three…"

The handle was heavy, but turned more smoothly than either of them had been expecting. After one complete revolution, the double-thick metal door swung open.

Inside was a thin, bright, bluish light. Zhou pushed Alex inside and then pulled the door closed behind them. The handle turned automatically as soon as it was shut, sealing with a faint hiss. On the opposite side of the room was another, even larger round metal door – the pod itself. For now, though, they were between the two, in the airlock that protected the main ship from the vacuum of space when the pod was deployed.

Zhou breathed a sigh of relief that they'd made it this far undetected. The sound was somehow dead inside the airlock, as if it had nowhere to go and so fell like a stone to the floor instead. Alex shivered to think of what would happen if they got stuck there – there obviously wasn't much oxygen and it would run out very quickly.

"What now?" Alex asked.

Zhou went to the small computer screen on the wall. Alex followed him, trying to make out what the buttons beside it meant. He watched as Zhou frowned at them and then consulted his phone.

"Well?" he asked.

Zhou shrugged. "Here goes," he said, before quickly pressing two buttons.

The second door – the one that led to the pod – began to open silently, moving smoothly but slowly. Zhou went to it and immediately stepped through. Alex followed – after all, it was too late to do anything else.

Inside, the pod looked like the cockpit of an aeroplane, except that it was spherical. There were two large, moulded seats in the middle, surrounded by angled banks of computer screens, keyboards, switches and buttons. Both seats were large and long, clearly built to fit the shape of a grey body. In front of each was what looked like a control stick.

What really made Alex take a sharp breath, though, was the view. The pod had a large window panel above the control console that stretched almost all the way around the craft. Through it, Alex and Zhou could see the hull of the alien ship, like a vast, cratered silver desert, stretching away into the distance. And below it, they could see the empty nothingness of space, pin-pricked by the bright lights of distant stars.

"Wow," said Alex.

"Yeah," said Zhou, his voice awed. "Pretty amazing. And look at the size of this ship. It's like a flying country, only with armour. If this thing got to Earth it'd be game over. We have *got* to get our data back to Task Force Alpha."

"Well, then," said Alex, "come on – you said you could fly this thing. Let's go!"

"Yeah," said Zhou, frowning as he sat down at the console. "I think I can."

"Don't think," said Alex, taking the other pilot's seat. "Just do it."

Zhou grinned. "Okay," he said, reaching for one of the switches and taking hold of the control stick in the other hand. "Hold on to your pants...."

Chapter 6

Under Attack

Zhou pressed the button. Instantly, lights began to run around the consoles as they turned on, blinking and glowing, some in colours that the boys could both recognize – green, red, yellow and blue – and others in colours they'd never seen before – some purple, but that were somehow also green, and others that were so different from anything they knew that they were indescribable.

There was a sound, too, a grating growl that overlaid the perpetual hum of the mother ship. "That's the engine!" said Zhou. "It must be! We're in business!"

Alex was gripping the arms of his seat so tightly that his fingers hurt. "What now?"

"I've got to find the docking release. It must be—"

Another sound began to blare, a loud, jarring screech like a police car siren but much louder and deeper. The light in the pod turned red, flashing angrily as it splashed all over everything.

"Turn it off!" Alex shouted, over the noise.

"I can't!" Zhou shouted back, "That's not the pod, that's the mother ship. They know we're here!"

"Then what do we do?" Alex asked, frantic.

"We make a run for it!" Zhou shouted back, pressing a button on the control stick.

There was a mechanical noise, like a clamp coming undone. The pod dropped into space. It hung there, floating, turning and tipping slowly so that the boys slid forward helplessly in their over-sized chairs.

"Fly!" Alex shouted. "We're sitting ducks! Make it fly!"

"I'm trying!" Zhou hollered, whacking his hand down on button after button, trying to get the pod to respond. "I haven't got time to look at–"

There was a zipping sound, and the pod righted itself, bobbing in zero gravity as if it were on a pond instead of hanging aimlessly.

"Yes!" Shouted Zhou, triumphant. "Now, if I–"

He pushed the controller up and the pod shot forwards, almost colliding with the mother ship looming around them. The boys shouted as Zhou pulled back and angled right. The pod shot away again, zooming out into the vastness of space and away from the ship.

"This is much easier than it looks!" Zhou shouted happily. "All I have to do is–"

"I don't care," Alex yelled at him. "Just get us home!"

Zhou opened his mouth to respond but before he could, there was an almighty explosion as something collided with their little ship. The pod shook violently. For a split second, Alex thought they had been blown up as outside, a huge fireball flared as brightly as the sun.

"They're firing at us," said Zhou, his face grim as he stared at a computer readout that he couldn't possibly understand. "That was close!"

"Well... do something!" said Alex.

"Like what?"

"I don't know – take evasive manoeuvres!"

Zhou shot him a killer glare. "This isn't *Star Trek,* you know. This is real!"

Another blast exploded outside. The weirdest thing was the lack of noise. Alex could see it and feel it as it buffeted the pod, but there was no sound except for what was going on inside their little spaceship.

"Why can't I hear anything?"

"Like what?" Zhou yelled, frantically pulling the pod to one side as another volley of silent fire shot past them and into the infinity of space.

"Outside," Alex said. "All those explosions – I can't hear them!"

Zhou grinned, "I told you – you've been watching too much TV. It's a vacuum out there – there's no sound in a vacuum! Sci-fi shows just put in loud explosions to make it more interesting!"

Alex stared out of the window, watching the silent eruptions go on and on, flowering like fiery blooms against the black void.

Zhou's right, he thought. *This* is *very different from a TV show.*

The silence was eerie. It was terrifying!

Outside, the mother ship was beginning to move, hauling its massive bulk after them. It looked like a mountain range, but moved so gracefully it hardly even shuddered.

"There must be a way home," Zhou said. "Alex, you're going to have to help me. Take my phone. Look for the video I took of that alien opening a portal."

Alex did as he was told, scrolling quickly through the record of their journey through the ship until he found the footage. "Now what?"

"Those buttons the alien pressed, to generate a wormhole between dimensions,"

Zhou said, adjusting the control stick slightly as the pod rocked. "See if the same ones are here on the pod control console anywhere."

Alex stood up, squinting at the video and then at the console. "I don't know," he said, "I can't see…."

"We've got incoming!" Zhou shouted. Alex looked up to see five small ships zipping towards them. "Find those buttons, Alex, or we're dead!"

Zhou yanked the control stick around, turning the pod so fast that Alex crashed sideways and bashed into the wall, losing his footing. He pulled himself upright as Zhou pushed the pod into a fast dive away from the mother ship, only to zip it around and under the hull again as he tried to avoid their pursuers. Out of the window, Alex could see bright streaks of light shooting past them and exploding as the grey ships fired on them.

"Hurry up!" Zhou shouted. "Sooner or later they're going to hit us and we'll explode like a firework!"

"I'm trying!" Alex shouted. "I can't see – no, wait – there's one! And another." He spotted the right buttons, a series of brightly coloured hexagons with strange markings on them. They were under a clear plastic cover, as if to stop them being pressed by accident. Alex flipped it up as a huge bang from the back of the pod nearly blew him off his feet, a shower of sparks exploding over both of them. The smell of metallic burning filled the air.

"Do it, Alex!" Zhou urged, "We're nearly finished!"

"I've got to make sure I get them in the right order," said Alex, trying to watch the video again as everything around him began to shake. He reached out, hand hovering over the controls. Five buttons, that's all it was. He took a deep breath and pressed them, firmly, as the grey fighters sent yet another volley of shots in their direction.

Nothing happened. Alex's heart was in his mouth – had he got the sequence wrong? Or didn't the portal work in a ship like this? Then, a blue flash of light appeared outside, flickering like a spinning whirlpool in the darkness of space. It spun, getting larger and larger – a wormhole, just like the one they'd seen earlier.

"You did it!" yelled Zhou, overjoyed. "Alex, you did it!"

"I don't know if it's going to be big enough," Alex shouted. "Look! It's not–"

They were hit again, this time by a streak of hot white light.

"We've got no choice," said Zhou, a serious look on his face. "I'm taking her in."

He pushed the control stick forward, and the pod zipped towards the spinning blue light. Alex sank into the chair again, holding on to it for dear life as the pod juddered and jumped.

Out of the window, Alex could see three flashes of bright light heading right towards them.

"Here we go!" Zhou shouted. "Aaargh!"

Chapter 7

Into the Wormhole

Zhou's cry rang through the space pod as they sped towards the spinning blue disc of energy. Alex's heart was in his mouth as the mother ship and alien fighters continued to fire at them, dazzling streaks of energy exploding outside the pod's window.

As they crossed the threshold of the wormhole, the pod was immediately swallowed by bright blue light. The vast emptiness of the universe vanished and was replaced by writhing, fluid energy, crackling and spitting white ripples of lightning towards the pod.

"We did it!" Zhou bellowed, "This is the first time a human has ever done this, Alex! We're making hist–"

There was a bright white flash of light outside and the pod juddered violently as the wormhole convulsed around them.

"What was that?" Alex asked, taking his seat and holding on to it.

"They're still firing at us – the aliens," Zhou said, with a frown, trying to hold the pod steady. "They're not–"

Something hit the back of the pod with such force that it was thrown into a hopeless spin. Both boys crashed out of their chairs as the craft up-ended, completely out of control. The light of the wormhole had turned from electric blue to pure white, as if a thousand lightning bolts had all hit at once.

Alex tried to cling on to a handle on the wall as the craft spun wildly out of control. It was like being inside a giant washing machine, turning over and over, faster and faster. As another blast hit, Alex lost his hold and felt himself lifted up, before slamming down a second later, right onto the control panel. He tried to struggle back to the handle, but before he could the pod had turned over again and he crashed to the floor, via a brief and painful visit to the ceiling.

Then, abruptly, something changed. The pod stopped turning over, levelling out. Outside, the bright light had vanished. Zhou dragged himself up and took the control stick, breathing hard.

"Are you OK?" He asked Alex. "Anything broken?"

"Don't think so," said Alex, crawling back into his seat. "What happened?"

They both looked out at the stars peppering the surrounding black – and there, hanging like a perfect blue and green marble in the hugeness of space, was Earth. The sphere curved away in front of them, protected by the faint bubble of atmosphere surrounding it. It was the most beautiful thing Alex had ever seen.

"Awesome!" he said.

"Yeah," nodded Zhou. "Quite a view. Pity we aren't a bit closer, though."

Alex tore his eyes away from the amazing sight of his home planet and turned to look at Zhou. "What do you mean?"

"The wormhole we opened – it should have taken us inside the atmosphere. After all, it did with the aliens, right? So why didn't it do that for us?"

Before Alex could think of an answer, Zhou pushed the control stick, turning the pod through 180 degrees.

"Oh…" Alex muttered, as the mouth of the wormhole floated into view. Except that it wasn't like a mouth anymore – it was a massive, jagged rip fizzing with angry white energy that burned like a molten volcano.

Zhou said something in Chinese that Alex didn't ask him to translate. He guessed it wasn't good.

"The energy discharged by the aliens firing into the wormhole must have made it expand," muttered Zhou. "This is really bad. Really, really bad."

Without another word he turned the pod back towards Earth and pushed the control stick forward to maximum thrust.

"What are you doing?" Alex asked, holding onto the side of his seat again.

"Sorry, but we're in for another bumpy ride. We've got to break through Earth's atmosphere – if we're not travelling fast enough, we'll just bounce off," Zhou explained. "It's going to get pretty warm in here. Let's just hope this thing's sturdy enough that we don't burn up on re-entry!"

Alex swallowed hard as Earth loomed larger and larger in front of them. He could see the whole continent of South America, from the snow-capped mountains of the Andes to the lush Amazon rainforest and the giant serpentine Amazon River cutting through Brazil, Colombia and Peru. He could even see the startling blue waters of the Caribbean, tiny islands shining like jewels dotted within it. He watched, slightly hypnotized, thinking that geography lessons would never be the same. The pod began to shudder.

"Here we go," said Zhou, gritting his teeth. "Hold on…"

Wisps of something that looked alarmingly like fire began to appear as they hit the atmosphere. The pod ploughed on, pushing through, shaking more and more violently. Zhou used both hands to keep it steady, forcing it through Earth's invisible barrier. He was right – it was getting warmer and warmer. Outside, the view of South America was replaced by a wall of heat and flame.

"I could do with some help, here!" Zhou shouted, as a roaring sound engulfed them. His arms were shaking with the effort of forcing the pod onwards.

Alex put his hands over Zhou's, both of them pushing against the resisting control stick. A second later there was a massive bang and the sound of electrical circuits shorting out. An acrid smell filled the air.

"Keep going!" Zhou yelled. "We have to get through, whatever it takes!"

As the pod burst through the flames, it gave one last, massive shudder – and everything died. All the lights on the control panels blinked out, and Alex felt the controls give up. There was no electronic hum, no sign of life at all. Silently, they leaned back in their chairs, the roaring outside now deafening. There was nothing more either of them could do.

The pod had cleared the atmosphere in one piece, but with nothing to control it. It plummeted like a stone. Alex had a moment to be thankful that they were heading towards the ocean, not land – and then to wonder whether that would make any difference at all, given that they had fallen all the way from space and didn't even have a parachute – before they hit.

The water came at them like a solid wall. They crashed into it and sank, down and down, so fast that in seconds the light from above was murky and green.

"What do we do now?" Alex asked, unable to keep the panic from his voice as his eyes strained to adjust to the darkness.

Zhou bit his lip, looking nervously at the glass of the pod's large window. "We hope that this thing can withstand a lot of pressure."

"And what if it can?" Alex asked, his voice frantic. "How much air have we got? Enough for us to work out how to fix this thing?"

Zhou didn't answer, getting out of his chair and going to the back of the pod, instead. Alex followed as, from his penknife, Zhou pulled out a tiny torch with a surprisingly strong beam. Handing it to Alex, he set about removing a smooth metal panel in the pod's wall. A wisp of smoke curled into the air as it came away. Alex stared at the mess of burned wires inside.

"I'm guessing that's a no, then," said Alex, feeling slightly sick.

"I don't even know where to begin," said Zhou. "Sorry."

"Let's – let's just open the pod door and swim for it!"

Zhou looked out of the window into the inky blackness of the water around them. He shook his head. "We can't. We must be pretty deep by now. The pressure would crush us. If we didn't drown first."

Alex swallowed, trying to quell his fear. "Great," he mumbled.

They floated down and down. After the insanity of the past few hours, it felt really weird. Suddenly they were like a bubble, drifting aimlessly on the breeze. Only if this bubble burst, they'd be dead instantly. And if it didn't…. Well, Alex tried not to think about that. If he did, he might go completely mad. He sat down in his chair and drew his knees up to his chin. It was getting colder and darker, and his teeth were beginning to chatter.

There was a gentle bump, and the pod came to rest, rocking slightly. Zhou leaned over the control panel to look through the darkened window. "We're in luck," he said. "Peak, not trench."

"Why is that lucky?" Alex asked, suddenly feeling very, very tired.

"Because if—"

Whatever Zhou had been about to explain was interrupted by a loud clang as something crunched into the top of the pod. They both yelled in fright, trying to see out into the pitch-black water outside. The pod began to move, as if it were being lifted by a huge, invisible hand.

Chapter 8

Countdown: Armageddon

"What was that?" Alex shouted. "What's happening?"

"I don't know," Zhou said, sounding as terrified as Alex felt. "That sounded like metal hitting us, but—"

His phone rang.

The two boys stared at each other for a moment. Then Zhou scrabbled to pull it out of his pocket. He peered at the screen in the gloom. "I can't believe it," he said. "I've got a signal!"

"Don't just stare at it!" Alex yelled, as the

pod carried on moving jerkily through the water. "Answer it!"

Zhou pressed the speaker button. A slightly tinny voice echoed into the pod.

"Mieville?" asked a girl's voice – Alex recognized it. It was Sasha!

"Asimov?" Zhou shouted. "Is that you?"

"Of course it's me," said the voice, "Is Bradbury with you?"

Zhou glanced at Alex. "Yes. We need help. We're in a space pod. We crashed, and now–"

"Mieville – zip it, would you? Just look out of the window."

The two boys looked up from the phone and into the darkness outside. They both gasped to see Sasha's face! She was sitting in the lit-up cab of what looked like a huge underwater tank. It had a crane on the top – the dangling grab of which cradled the pod.

It was Sasha who had grabbed them! As they watched, she raised one hand and waved with a grin.

"Sorry if I scared you, boys," she said. "Let's get you back to base, shall we?"

"Listen," said Zhou, urgently. "There's something you need to know. About the greys. They–"

"We know," said Sasha. "We saw the wormhole rip open. And good work – the auto-sync downloaded all the data you collected as soon as you were in range. The scientists are looking at it now. Stop talking, save your air. Asimov out."

Sasha turned the tank around, driving slowly back along the tracks she had made in the ocean's sediment.

"Bradbury?" Alex asked, after a moment. "Why did she call me that? I'm Alex Jones, not Bradbury."

"It's a code name," Zhou told him. "We've all got them. I'm Mieville, Sasha's Asimov. You're Bradbury. You're one of the team now!"

Ahead of them, something was looming out of the ocean floor. At first Alex thought it was an underwater mountain range, but then he noticed that whatever it was had windows – there were squares of light dotted all over it.

"What on Earth is that?"

Zhou grinned. "That is Task Force Alpha's base. Looks like we landed in the right spot."

They carried on driving right up to the massive structure, which towered above them. Alex realized that what they were facing was a giant metal wall that definitely wasn't natural – or made by humans. In fact, it looked distinctly like the outside of the alien mother ship, although not quite as big.

"Wait," Alex said. "Wait a minute – is this…?"

"Yup," said Zhou. "It's another alien spaceship. It's been down here for who knows how long. Probably before we humans started moving about upstairs. The military found it a few months ago, and have been trying to learn about it ever since. Made sense to have Task Force Alpha's base here, once the aliens started organizing for an attack."

The tank drove into the ship and two huge barriers lowered behind them. Slowly, the water began to drain away, until both the tank and the space pod were open to the air. Zhou and Alex hurried to open the pod door, scrambling outside to catch their breath as Sasha climbed down from the tank.

"Where are we anyway?" asked Alex.

"At the bottom of the Atlantic Ocean," Zhou replied. "Right in the centre of the Bermuda Triangle, in fact"

"Bermuda Triangle!" exclaimed Alex. "Is this why all those weird things happened right here?"

"We think so, but–"

"Hey you two," Sasha yelled. "Move it. We've got to get to command and control. The attack's started already!"

Command and control, when they got there, was in chaos. Alex couldn't remember ever being as glad to see other people – there were soldiers everywhere, all dressed in camouflage gear, bustling about or busy at controls. The military had rigged up huge banks of computers and screens to replace the alien technology, and on the largest was an image of the huge, gaping wormhole.

Five small alien ships – the ones that had chased Alex and Zhou, hovered in front of it.

There was a loud crackle, and a strange, scratchy voice spoke into the air.

"The broadcast is starting again, sir," barked one of the soldiers, her hand instinctively tapping a button as she looked at the screen. "English, this time."

"Humans. Release the hostages and return our vessels. You have thirty minutes to comply. Humans. Release the hostages and return our vessels. You have thirty minutes to comply…"

"Hostages?" Alex whispered to Zhou, "what do they mean, hostages?"

Zhou shrugged and shook his head.

"General O'Neill, sir, Asimov reporting for duty," snapped out Sasha, sharply, to a tall, stern-looking man who was staring at the screen. "Mieville and Bradbury have returned safely."

The man turned to look at them with a nod. "Glad you made it back. Looks as if the aliens learnt human language from you. They're talking to us in English and Chinese."

"Sir, what are we going to do?" Zhou asked.

"Well, we can't give them this ship," said the general, turning to look back at the screen.

"Why not?" Alex asked, and then added a quick, "Sir," just to be on the safe side.

"Even if we could get this thing fully operational, we can't move it," Sasha told him. "Look at the size of it. It'd cause massive tidal waves, bigger than anything we've ever seen before. Most of Earth's landmass would be submerged."

"Then – what about the hostages they're talking about?" Alex asked. "That's probably the crew of this ship, isn't it? Are they still here, somewhere?"

"Son, this ship has been down here for thousands, probably millions of years," said the general. "Anything that was alive has long since crumbled into dust."

"But–"

"We don't have a choice," the general interrupted. "We can't give them what they want and so they're bound to attack. We have to fire on them before they fire on us. Perhaps then they'll think twice about invading. Prepare the missiles."

"Aye sir, preparing missiles," barked a soldier.

"No – wait! Just wait a second," said Alex, thinking fast.

"We don't have a second, Alex," said the general. "We have to act, now."

Zhou put a hand on Alex's arm. "He's right. We've seen how big that mother ship is. We have to stop it somehow."

"But, shouldn't we at least try to communicate with them? What if they don't know?" Alex said. "What if they don't know that we can't give the ship back? What if they don't understand what will happen to Earth?"

"What do they care?" Sasha asked, "They were going to invade anyway!"

"You don't know that!" said Alex, frantically. "The greys in those space pods haven't attacked us. They're trying to talk to us! You said this ship was only found a few months ago. You turned things on, didn't you? Maybe it's been lost for all those years, and when you turned it on, it sent a signal. Like… like Zhou's homing beacon!"

"Maybe he's got a point," Zhou said. "The greys didn't start appearing until we moved aboard this ship, did they? Maybe they're just looking for the ship, and their crew."

"Yes!" cried Alex. "Maybe they're just trying to get their people to safety! Perhaps all they've been doing up until now is trying to–"

"Missiles in place, sir. Standby…."

"We can't let this happen," shouted Alex. "We have to talk to them first. If we fire at them, they'll definitely come and destroy us. Look what they did to the wormhole – and they weren't even trying! You'll be starting a war, general – no doubt about it. And not just a world war, but an intergalactic one!"

"Missiles ready to launch, general."

The general held up a finger, still staring at the screen. "On my mark…"

"Wait!" shouted Alex again, desperately. "Don't!"

Chapter 9

The Ultimatum

Alex held his breath as he looked at General O'Neill. He knew he was right – he just knew it. They couldn't fire on the greys. They had to find another way.

The general stared at Alex hard for a moment. Then he nodded curtly. "All right," he said, "We'll give it a shot."

Sasha clutched Alex's arm with a grin. "You did it," she said quietly. "Good job!"

"Don't celebrate just yet," Zhou whispered. "Let's see whether the greys listen to us, first."

Alex let out the breath he'd been holding as around them, command and control sprang into life.

"Weapons, I want all missile batteries on standby, just in case," barked General O'Neill. "Communications, can we broadcast to them?"

"Yes sir," snapped out another soldier, sharply. "The aliens will hear you loud and clear."

"All right then," said the general, "Let's do this."

Everyone fell into a tense silence as the general spoke into the air.

"This is General O'Neill, of Earth," he began. "We welcome you to our airspace. We would like our two peoples to work together, in peace."

There was a pause as a crackle interrupted the general's speech. Alex looked over to the communications officer and saw him nod at the general.

"They're listening, sir," he mouthed. "Incoming transmission–"

"Humans," came the alien voice they had heard before, booming into the command centre. "There can be no peace until you have returned our vessel and the hostages."

"We are holding no hostages," replied the general. "And I regret to say that we cannot return the vessel."

"Then our warning still stands," responded the voice, immediately. "The thirty minutes are almost up."

"Wait," said the general. "Please. If there was a way to return your ship to you, I assure you we would. But doing so would cause devastation to our planet. We are not refusing to return it – we simply cannot. Do you understand?"

There was a tense pause as the grey seemed to think about what the general had said. Alex wondered whether the aliens were all standing around on their ship, just like the humans, discussing what to do.

"I understand your words, general. Our own scientists will assess the likely damage to Earth," came the grey voice. "If what you say is untrue, we will have no choice but to retrieve the vessel by force. You will return the hostages now."

"We have no hostages," the general repeated, frustrated.

"You must return the crew of the vessel you are now occupying," insisted the grey, in the same strange, flat voice.

"There are no creatures of your kind here," said O'Neill. "This vessel was empty when we found it. We believe it crashed thousands of years ago. As far as we know there were no survivors."

There was another pause. Then, "Our scientists request two hours to assess the damage to your planet," said the grey, calmly. "In that time you will return our people to us."

"But–" began the general, but there was another crackle. The greys had broken the connection.

"Well, that went well," said Zhou. "I guess we have at least another two hours to live."

General O'Neill was barking orders again. "Make sure we are fully armed from this point. Back-up will be here in six hours, we'll have to pray we have enough firepower to down their ships first. All weapons to target that wormhole. Send immediate alerts to world leaders to prepare their populations for an imminent attack."

"Wait," said Alex, speaking up, "what about finding the other greys?"

The general turned and, with an air of tired patience, spoke to him. "Son, our scientists have been all over this bird, and there are no living creatures here. None. Whatever our outer-space visitors think, there are no greys here. We've been given a period of grace, and by heck I'm going to use it. Now, I think it was time you children were returned to your families. We thank you for all you've done, but your assistance is no longer needed."

He nodded to a soldier standing nearby and Alex, Sasha and Zhou were escorted from command and control, out into the cold corridor beyond.

"It's for the best," said the soldier who led them away. The name tag sewn on his camo shirt read 'Carter'. "You kids have been great, but you should be with your families now. We'll get you on the tug and up to one of the transports up top. They'll have you home in no time."

"Not in the next two hours!" muttered Alex sulkily.

"Look, we can still be helpful, Sam," said Sasha, who obviously knew the soldier.

"Yeah," said Zhou. "After all, Alex and I are the only people who have actually seen the inside of a grey ship! And we've flown one! Doesn't that count for something?"

Carter looked down at them and smiled. "It counts for a lot. But you're still going home. General's orders."

Chapter 10

Escape Route

Alex's mind was racing. The greys were convinced that they had people of their own, somewhere on this ship. He also knew General O'Neill wasn't lying – he genuinely believed that this ship was empty. But surely the greys on the mother ship would have scanned for their own kind, or something. So if there really were greys here, they must be hidden somewhere…. He stopped abruptly. Sasha and Zhou turned to look at him.

"I know where they are," he said.

"What?" asked Sasha.

"The greys. The greys that were in this ship when it crashed. I know where they are."

"What are you talking about, Alex?" Zhou asked. "You heard the general – they've already searched the ship."

"They haven't," said Alex. "They believe they have, but they haven't. Think about it – it's obvious really. If you were in a boat, a normal boat, and you knew it was going to sink – what would you do?"

"Get into a lifeboat," said Sasha. "But there aren't any in a–" She stopped, her eyes widening, and Alex knew she'd got it too. "The space pods!"

He nodded. "That's where they are. The ship was crashing, so they went for the space pods to escape. But it crashed before they could use them, and they were stuck there."

Zhou shook his head. "You're right," he said, "You're actually right! The space pods are attached to the lower levels – the ones that took the brunt of the crash. They were flooded so the first exploration teams sealed them off, to make the rest of the ship safe. Everyone assumed there would be no survivors down there."

The three of them looked up at their escort. "Well?" Sasha demanded, "Come on, Sam, you know that must be right! We have to go and look."

Sam shook his head. "Sorry, kids. I'm to escort you off this ship and get you home. Leave this to the professionals."

"The professionals are going to get us all killed!" Alex yelled.

"Now, wait a minute…" said Sam, annoyed.

"Sam," said Sasha. "I'm really sorry about this. I'll make it up to you, I promise."

"Make what up to me?" Sam asked, perplexed.

"This," said Sasha, before she let loose a flying kick at his shin. Her hard boots impacted Sam's leg and he yelled, crumpling to the floor. "Run!" she cried.

Alex and Zhou didn't need telling twice. They took off down the corridor after Sasha, Sam's angry yells following them all the way.

"We've got to be quick," Sasha said, breathlessly, "he's really hard-core – he'll be back on his feet before we know it! We need to head for the tank."

They crashed through the exit door and Zhou clanged it closed behind them, spinning the handle so that it shut firmly. Sasha ran up to the huge underwater vehicle and dragged open the door with both hands.

"They'll probably throw us in jail for life for this, but I think you're right, Alex," she said. "This might be the only shot we've got at stopping the greys destroying the planet!"

They clambered inside, crawling quickly into their seats. Alex looked around – the inside of the tank was full of equipment – heavy-duty diving suits, computer equipment, mechanical gadgets. It looked big from outside, but inside it was cramped. There was hardly room to move.

"Incoming!" Zhou yelled, as Sasha started the engine. Through the ultra-thick windscreen they could see Sam – he'd made it through the door and was stumbling down the steps towards them.

"Well," said Sasha, pushing the tank forward, "he'd better give up, or he's going to get very wet...."

Water started pouring into the holding bay as the soldier ran at them, shouting and waving. Soon he was wading through rising water.

"Go back," Sasha yelled, through the windscreen. "Don't be an idiot! Go back!"

She rolled the tank forward, turning it around, and Alex and Zhou craned their necks to watch as Sam finally gave up and retreated.

"Is he OK?" Sasha asked, concentrating on driving the tank.

"He'll be fine," said Zhou. "We won't be, if you two are wrong about this, but Sam'll be fine!"

"I'm right," Alex said, quietly, as they rolled out of the now-filled hangar and onto the uneven, rocky ocean floor. "I know I am."

"Even if you are," said Zhou, "what are we going to do if they're all dead? Which they must be, mustn't they? After all this time?"

"We'll cross that bridge," Sasha muttered, "when we come to—"

There was a loud clunk, and the tank lurched to one side. All three of them yelled in fright.

"What was that?" Alex shouted, as Sasha grappled with the controls, trying to pull the vehicle back on course. She was too busy trying to stop the tank from sliding to answer his question. The back wheels skidded, pulled by some unknown force.

"It's a landslide," Zhou realized, tapping the screen that picked out the terrain around them in glowing green lines. "There, look – that crevice. The edges are crumbling and we got too close."

"Don't panic," said Sasha, with gritted teeth. "This old girl can get out of it. Just... don't... panic...."

There was another clunk as the tank's wheel clawed up a large rock before it crumbled away into the abyss.

"How deep is the crevice?" Alex asked, fearfully.

"Best not to think about that," advised Zhou.

The tank jerked again, forwards this time, and then the engine coughed, loudly, as Sasha fought to find a gear. And then it began to roll along level ground again, as if nothing had happened.

"There," said Sasha, with a sigh of relief. "All fine. You boys are such worriers!"

"Sasha," said Zhou, quietly, ignoring her jibe and looking at another screen. "Put the searchlights on."

Sasha did. Two huge, white lights burst into life, casting the ocean floor in steely greys and deep greens. Shoals of pale fish, disturbed by the sudden burst of white light, skittered away, disappearing into the darkness like flurries of snowflakes.

Ahead of them, they could see the edge of the downed ship, tilting at a sharp angle where its hull had crushed itself against the Earth. The wall-thick metal had crumpled like paper, creating strange, rigid ripples that radiated out from where the hull rested on the ocean floor. Just above the impact zone, close to the rocky mantel, there they were – Alex recognized them immediately. The exposed, semi-circular shapes of the ship's space pods, set in a line – and all intact.

"Right," said Sasha. "Let's take a closer look, see if we've got any visitors."

Sasha drove the tank right up to the first pod. She angled one of the searchlights, bringing the mechanical arm it was set in down so that it was right outside the pod's window. The light illuminated the inside of the little ship.

Alex's heart sank. It was empty.

"Ok," said Sasha, with a sigh. "Let's try the next one…"

No luck. That pod was empty, too – and it wasn't third time lucky, either, as the one beside it was also distressingly free of aliens. Alex was just about to give up, when–

"Look," shouted Zhou. "Look!"

Sure enough, there, in the fourth pod, were not one but two greys strapped into their seats. Alex stared at them through the murky glass – their bodies, as far as Alex could tell, were intact, which was good. At least, he thought, we can prove that we didn't kill them ourselves, and that we haven't experimented on them, or anything horrible like that….

"Great," said Sasha, "Ok, we've done the easy bit. Now we've got to hope our clamp is strong enough to pull that pod out of there without crushing it."

Sasha carefully manoeuvred the tank's huge mechanical grab on to the embedded sphere, and it came out surprisingly easily – almost as if it wasn't part of the bigger ship at all. Sasha reversed the tank until she could set the pod on the rocky seabed.

"That's weird," said Alex. "When we took our pod from the mother ship, it had to disengage."

"Well," said Zhou, thoughtfully, "We know they were trying to escape the crash, and they'd left it really late. Perhaps the pods had already come loose, but the pilots didn't have time to fly them out of their docks before the ship crashed?"

Sasha was moving the tank again, edging closer to the little round spacecraft. "Let's not worry about that now," she said. "How are we doing for time?"

Alex checked his watch. "Only 35 minutes until the deadline."

"Well, then, let's–"

Sasha broke off as a bright blue light exploded around them. It shot down through the watery depths and completely enveloped the pod – and, still standing beside it, the tank.

"Back up," Zhou shouted, shielding his eyes. "Sasha – reverse!"

Sasha rolled the tank back a little. As they watched, the pod began to move. At first it just rocked slightly, but then it began to rise, drifting up the shaft of blue light like a bubble.

"What's happening?" Alex asked, amazed.

"I don't know, but it's got to be the greys, hasn't it? I guess they knew exactly where their people were – they just couldn't get to them." Sasha muttered. "Zhou – turn on the tank's radio. I turned it off so command and control couldn't call us, but they might know what's going on."

Zhou flicked a switch on the tank's dashboard. Immediately the radio buzzed into life, soldiers on the larger ship barking Sasha and Zhou's call signs as they tried to get them to respond.

"Asimov here, come in," Sasha said, snatching up the handset and speaking into it.

"Asimov, this is Task Force Alpha base."

"Reading you," said Sasha, shortly. "Do you see what we see? We freed one of the pods and…"

"We see it, Asimov," the soldier interrupted. "The greys have started the attack with a laser beam, but at present we don't seem to be hit–"

"No, sir, they're not attacking!" cried Sasha. "We found a pod containing greys and they're collecting them somehow… sort of… beaming them up," she said, raising an eyebrow at Zhou and Alex.

"Wait, we're receiving another communication from them," the soldier said. "Yes, yes, they're confirming what you said… they're collecting the alien crew… they say there are more of them down there."

Alex, Sasha and Zhou looked out at the other pods lined up along the ship's hull. "Understood, base," said Sasha, "Tell them we're working on it!"

It took them almost half an hour to free the other pods from their docks, the alien beam retrieving each one. Alex just hoped that the greys wouldn't blame them for the fact their comrades were dead.

"That's it, base," Sasha said, into the handset. "That's all the pods. We're coming back. Asimov out."

"What if the grey scientists' findings go against ours?" Alex asked, as they bumped and slid their way back towards the hangar.

Zhou glanced at him, and for once he wasn't grinning. He shrugged.

Alex didn't want to think about it either, staring out of the window into the dark murky water, instead. Everything seemed slightly unreal – even more so than it had when they were in space. They were going to be in massive trouble back at base.

"Hey, buckle up, cowboy," said Sasha, glancing at him. "You did a good job. You might just have saved Earth, you know!"

Alex tried to grin back. Then he spotted something outside the window. "Hey," he said, "What's that?"

It was a large, long black bulk, connected to the Task Force Alpha base.

"It's the super sub," Zhou frowned. "We used it when we first visited the base. It's reinforced to deal with the pressure at this level, and built so that it can connect seamlessly to the ship. It's how they transport personnel to and from the surface."

They rolled along the length of the sub into the tank's holding bay, jumping out the minute the water had subsided. Getting out of the tank was like taking out earplugs – suddenly every sound was louder and closer. Their boots rang against the wet metal as they scrambled up the steps.

Bursting into the corridor, they were faced with a furious-looking General O'Neill.

"Follow me," he barked, heading off down the narrow walkway.

"What's happening?" Sasha cried as two soldiers ran past her carrying equipment.

"We're evacuating," the general shouted back. "Get yourselves aboard the sub." Ahead, a red light glowed above a small hatch. The running soldiers climbed through it and another soldier stood, waving them on and yelling.

"Didn't we do enough?" Sasha asked.

O'Neill spun to look at them with a mixture of anger and respect on his face. "Yeah, you did enough. They're not going to fire on us or remove the ship. But they don't want us to use it, either. So they're sealing it. We were given ten minutes to evacuate our personnel and equipment." As he finished speaking, a computer terminal in the wall beside them burst into flames. Bitter electrical fumes mingled with the ship's already fuggy atmosphere.

"They're making sure we can't use their technology," Zhou added, wide-eyed.

"General, sir," the soldier interrupted, "all crew members have been accounted for. You're the last ones through."

Alex crawled into the hatch, watching as it sealed behind them with a mixture of relief and sadness. He gazed silently out of the window until the alien ship finally vanished from view. After all, it was probably the last one he'd ever see.

Epilogue

Two days later, Alex, Sasha and Zhou were
still in the Bermuda Triangle –
but on the surface, rather than in its
depths. The sub had taken them to an
aircraft carrier – a huge edifice more like
a city than a ship. It floated gently on
the flecked blue and green glass of the
Atlantic Ocean.

The past two days had been full of
debriefs. Alex and Zhou explained exactly
what happened aboard the mother ship, as
well as what they had seen and heard.
Sasha was disciplined for disobeying direct
orders, even though she wasn't even really

in the military. She didn't seem too bothered by the telling off, though.

Finally the interviews had ended and the three of them stood on the deck, enjoying the hot sunshine. They could still see the rip that the wormhole had created, but the small grey ships had gone, as had the blue beam. And, slowly, the wormhole was disappearing, too, sewing itself together. Soon there would be no sign that it had ever even been there.

"Well," said Sasha, leaning on the rail. "That's that, then."

"I wonder why they were here?" Zhou mused. "The first time, I mean, when they crashed."

"I think they were explorers," said Alex. "They just came through the wormhole to see what was here."

Sasha shrugged. "Well, let's hope they don't ever get curious again."

"If they do," General O'Neill's voice came from behind them, "At least they'll be able to understand us. Thanks to you three."

"What happens now, general?" asked Sasha, turning to look up at him. "Do we just… go home?"

The general smiled. "Not quite. We thought you all deserved a holiday, after all you've done," he said. "You ever been to Florida, Alex?"

Alex's eyes widened. "Er – no, sir."

"They call it the Sunshine State. Sun, sea, sand…"

"Alligators," Zhou added, and Sasha dug him in the ribs.

"Think you might like it?"

"Yes, sir!" said Alex and Sasha together.

"Oh – and look who's come to keep you company," added O'Neill, as a helicopter came into land, and several people jumped out.

Alex squinted into the bright sun, trying to make out who they were.

"Mum," he yelled, after a moment, amazed that she was there. "Mum!"

And then, as he hurried over to her, Alex realized that he recognized one of the other people, too. He was tanned browner than a nut and limping slightly, but he was actually there.

"Hello, Alex," said his dad. "Sounds as if you've got a bit of a story to tell me, eh?"

THE END

FICTION EXPRESS

THE READERS TAKE CONTROL!

Have you ever wanted to change the course of a plot, change a character's destiny, tell an author what to write next?

Well, now you can!

'Shadow People' was originally written for the award-winning interactive e-book website Fiction Express.

Fiction Express e-books are published in gripping weekly episodes. At the end of each episode, readers are given voting options to decide where the plot goes next. They vote online and the winning vote is then conveyed to the author who writes the next episode, in real time, according to the readers' most popular choice.

www.fictionexpress.co.uk

FICTION EXPRESS

TALK TO THE AUTHORS

The Fiction Express website features a blog where readers can interact with the authors while they are writing. An exciting and unique opportunity!

FANTASTIC TEACHER RESOURCES

Each weekly Fiction Express episode comes with a PDF of teacher resources packed with ideas to extend the text.

"The teaching resources are fab and easily fill a whole week of literacy lessons!"
Rachel Humphries, teacher at Westacre Middle School

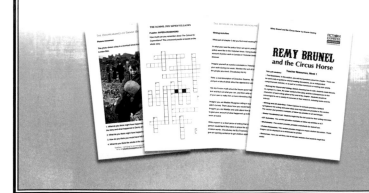

FICTI●N EXPRESS

My Cousin Faustina
by Bea Davenport

Jez is horrified to find a strange girl sitting in his kitchen when he gets home from school. His parents claim she is a distant cousin, but Jez senses something odd about her. Just what dark secret is Faustina hiding?

In his quest to find out, Jez learns the true value of family and friendship.

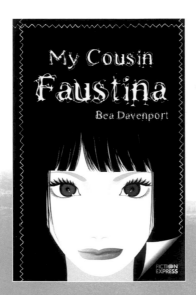

ISBN 978-1-78322-539-2

FICTI☻N EXPRESS

The Time Detectives:
The Mystery of Maddie Musgrove
by Alex Woolf

When Joe Smallwood goes to stay with his Uncle Theo and cousin Maya life seems dull, until he finds a strange smartphone nestling beside a gravestone. The phone enables Joe and Maya to become time-travelling detectives and takes them on an exciting adventure back to Victorian times. Can they prove maidservant Maddie Musgrove's innocence? Can they save her from the gallows?

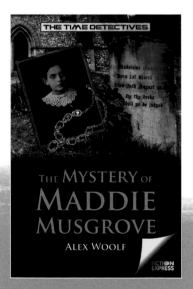

ISBN 978-1-783-22459-3

FICTI●N EXPRESS

The Time Detectives:
The Disappearance of Danny Doyle
by Alex Woolf

When the Time Detectives, Joe and Maya, stumble upon an old house in the middle of a wood, its occupant has a sad tale to tell. Michael was evacuated to Dorset during World War II with his twin brother, Danny. While there, Danny mysteriously disappeared and was never heard from again. Can Joe and Maya succeed where the police failed, journey back to 1941 and trace Michael's missing brother?

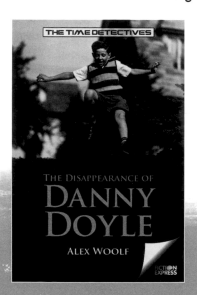

THE TIME DETECTIVES

THE DISAPPEARANCE OF
DANNY
DOYLE

ALEX WOOLF

FICTION EXPRESS

ISBN 978-1-783-22458-6

FICTION EXPRESS

The School for Supervillains
by Louie Stowell

Mandrake DeVille is heading to St Luthor's School for Supervillains, where a single act of kindness lands you in the detention pit, and only lying, cheating bullies get top marks. On paper, Mandrake's a model student: her parents are billionaire supervillains, and she has superpowers. The trouble is, Mandrake secretly wants to save the world, not destroy it.

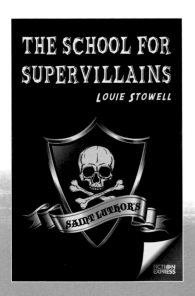

ISBN 978-1-783-22460-9

FICTION EXPRESS

Mind Swap
by Alex Woolf

Simon Archer is a bully. He's nasty to his classmates, his teachers, his mum. Then, one morning, Simon looks in the mirror and gets a shock. The face staring back at him is not his own. Who did this to him? And will anyone ever believe who he really is?

Simon's body has changed – but can he ever change inside?

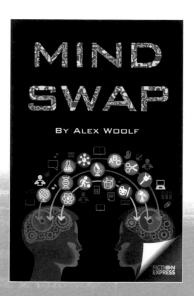

ISBN 978-1-783-22550-7

About the Author

Sharon and her husband live in a remote village in northern England, surrounded by fells and sheep. When she's not writing, she bakes a lot of cakes and bread, attempts to grow things in an allotment, and catches the baby rabbits unhelpfully brought in by the cat.